Ex-Library: Friends of
Lake County Public Library

Mouse TV

A Richard Jackson Book

by Matt Novak

Orchard Books / New York

LAKE COUNTY PUBLIC LIBRARY

3 3113 01458 6962

Copyright © 1994 by Matt Novak
All rights reserved. No part of this book may be reproduced or transmitted in any form or by
any means, electronic or mechanical, including photocopying, recording, or by any information
storage or retrieval system, without permission in writing from the Publisher.

Orchard Books, 95 Madison Avenue, New York, NY 10016

Manufactured in the United States of America. Printed by Barton Press, Inc. Bound by
Horowitz/Rae. The text of this book is set in 24 point Korinna. The illustrations are acrylic
paintings reproduced in full color. 10 9 8 7 6 5 4 3 2

Library of Congress Cataloging-in-Publication Data
Novak, Matt. Mouse TV / by Matt Novak. p. cm. "A Richard Jackson book"—Half t.p.
Summary: Each member of the Mouse family wants to watch something different on television,
but they discover a solution to their problem one night when the television does not work.
ISBN 0-531-06856-0. ISBN 0-531-08706-9 (lib. bdg.)
[1. Television—Fiction. 2. Family life—Fiction. 3. Mice—Fiction.] I. Title.
PZ7.N867Mo 1994 [E]—dc20 93-49399

Whenever the mouse family gathered around their TV, they could never agree on what to watch.

Papa Mouse wanted
action and adventure,

but Mama Mouse
wanted comedy.

Laszlo loved history,

but Emily loved mystery.

  "Science for me," said Pinky.

"Scary stuff for me," said Melba.

  "Music! Music!" cried Sally.

"Games! Games!" shouted Elmer.

"The how-to channel," yelled Hilda.

"The where-to channel," howled Zeke.

They argued loudest during the commercials

and always woke up the baby.

But one night the TV did not work.
"What do we do now?" asked Papa.

So they explored

and made things.

They played games

and sang songs.

They made scary faces

and performed experiments.

They put on a play

and danced funny dances.

When it was bedtime, Papa read a story
of action and adventure.

They all agreed it was a wonderful story, and best of all . . .

there were no commercials.